LIFE IN THE
DOGHOUSE

Elmer and the
Talent Show

DANNY ROBERTSHAW & RON DANTA

Written by Crystal Velasquez • Illustrated by Laura Catrinella

ALADDIN New York London Toronto Sydney New Delhi

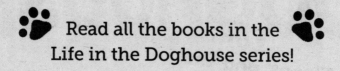 Read all the books in the Life in the Doghouse series!

Elmer and the Talent Show

Moose and the Smelly Sneakers

Coming soon:

Millie, Daisy, and the Scary Storm

Elmer and the Talent Show

🐾 ALADDIN

An imprint of Simon & Schuster Children's Publishing Division

1230 Avenue of the Americas, New York, New York 10020

First Aladdin paperback edition February 2022

Text copyright © 2022 by Danny Robertshaw and Ron Danta

Illustrations copyright © 2022 by Laura Catrinella

Photographs on pages 133–137 by Val Evans Moore

Also available in an Aladdin hardcover edition.

All rights reserved, including the right of reproduction in whole or in part in any form.

ALADDIN and related logo are registered trademarks of Simon & Schuster, Inc.

For information about special discounts for bulk purchases, please contact

Simon & Schuster Special Sales at 1-866-506-1949 or business@simonandschuster.com.

The Simon & Schuster Speakers Bureau can bring authors to your live event. For more information or to book an event contact the Simon & Schuster Speakers Bureau at 1-866-248-3049 or visit our website at www.simonspeakers.com.

Designed by Tiara Iandiorio

The illustrations for this book were rendered digitally.

The text of this book was set in Museo Slab.

Manufactured in the United States of America 1221 OFF

10 9 8 7 6 5 4 3 2 1

Names: Velasquez, Crystal, writer. | Robertshaw, Danny, author. | Danta, Ron, author. | Catrinella, Laura, illustrator.

Title: Elmer and the talent show / Danny Robertshaw, Ron Danta ; written by Crystal Velasquez ; illustrated by Laura Catrinella.

Description: First Aladdin paperback edition. | New York : Aladdin, 2022. |

Series: Life in the doghouse | Audience: Ages 7 to 10. |

Summary: Elmer is a special needs dachshund who lives at Danny & Ron's Rescue, but he longs to be adopted, and when he attracts the attention of a family, he is willing to do anything to impress them—including working hard at the agility course for the pet talent show.

Identifiers: LCCN 2021046630 (print) | LCCN 2021046631 (ebook) | ISBN 9781534482616 (paperback) | ISBN 9781534482609 (hardcover) | ISBN 9781534482623 (ebook)

Subjects: LCSH: Dachshunds—Juvenile fiction. | Dog adoption—Juvenile fiction. | Dogs—Agility trials—Juvenile fiction. | Human-animal relationships—Juvenile fiction. | CYAC: Dachshunds—Fiction. | Dogs—Fiction. | Dog adoption—Fiction. | Human-animal relationships—Fiction.

Classification: LCC PZ7.V4877 El 2022 (print) | LCC PZ7.V4877 (ebook) | DDC 813.6 [Fic]—dc23

LC record available at https://lccn.loc.gov/2021046630

LC ebook record available at https://lccn.loc.gov/2021046631

To all the other Elmers in the world who
need someone to give them a chance.

This book wouldn't be possible without our
genetic love for animals given to us by our
parents and brought to life by one who saw
more in us than we ever saw in ourselves:
Ron Davis.

Chapter 1

ELMER LOVED LOTS of things—belly rubs, ear scratches, squishy toys that squeaked when he chewed on them. But his favorite was definitely hearing the *scoop, scoop* sound that meant Danny and Ron, the humans who ran the dog rescue where he lived, were awake and making breakfast.

"Good morning, Elmer!" Danny unlatched

Elmer's crate and put a silver bowl filled with food inside. Elmer gave Danny's hand a quick lick and wagged his tail before he started eating. "Aw, I love you, too," Danny said.

Buster, the brown-and-white basset hound with the droopy eyes, was still snoring away in a bed by the fireplace. But most of the others stirred the moment the light in the kitchen blinked on. Elmer could hear Lucy's high-pitched yip from the crate above his and Momo's satisfied snuffles and grunts from the end of the hallway. Elmer wasn't the only one who loved digging in to the feast every morning, but he was one of the few who had to have special food that was soft and easy to chew.

After breakfast Danny opened the dogs' crates and led them to the backyard.

"All right, go play!" he said, his grin crinkling the corners of his blue eyes.

Elmer didn't hesitate. He liked showing Danny and Ron how good he was at running across the fresh green grass, with his long hair blowing in the wind. On his little dachshund legs, he could run even faster than Joey, the Jack Russell terrier.

Elmer trotted around the large yard, stopping only long enough to sniff Charlie the Chihuahua and bat a lime-green tennis ball with his paws. All the playing made him thirsty. Most days were pretty sunny and hot in South Carolina, but Danny and Ron made sure the dogs had lots of shady spots to rest and plenty to drink. Elmer padded over to one of the bowls of water that were tucked against the side of the redbrick house. After lapping up a few sips, he peered down into the bowl. When the ripples stilled, he could see his own reflection in the water. He had been born with a misshapen mouth that made it hard to eat, and not long ago, he could barely see out of his right eye. It took six surgeries and weeks of wearing a cone around his neck, but the doctors had fixed his jaw and saved his eye. His lips no longer closed,

he was missing teeth, and his long tongue hung from the side of his mouth. But he had survived.

Ron and Danny told Elmer all the time that he was a good boy, a beautiful dog who would find his forever home any day now. But when he looked at himself, he wasn't so sure. After all, why would anyone adopt him when they could take home Lady, the adorable gold-colored corgi, or the litter of five-month-old German shepherds—Huey, Dewey, and Louie—who were so tiny when they first got to the rescue that they had to be fed with a baby bottle? People usually wanted the puppies—or at least cute dogs who didn't need surgery just to straighten their snout.

But Elmer tried not to let that get him down. He knew he was lucky to be with Danny and

Ron. After all, not many horse trainers would turn their own home into a dog rescue, but years ago, that's just what they did. When they weren't teaching riders how to lead horses through a series of jumps during competitions, they started helping dogs who needed them. At first they saved just a few pups who had lost their homes in a hurricane and were all alone in the world. Danny and Ron set aside space for the dogs in their horse stables, then nursed them back to health, and found them loving families. But soon the numbers grew and grew, and the horse stables weren't enough. So their dining room table became rows of crates. Instead of stacking logs in their fireplace, they filled it with dog beds, and stocked their pantry with kibble. Eventually, their house had more dogs than people. They often said that they were only guests now in the dogs' house.

Elmer loved life at the rescue. There were always lots of pups—and sometimes cats—to play with, nobody minded if he jumped up on the sofa in the living room, and when it rained outside and he got scared, Danny would sit beside him and stroke his long soft ears until he fell asleep. Like most of the animals in the house, Elmer remembered what it was like to live in a place where he wasn't safe. Here, Elmer knew he would be taken care of, no matter what. Still, that didn't change the fact that his dearest wish in the world was for some nice people to take him home and make him part of their family.

He lay on his back, cushioned by the soft grass, imagining what that would be like. As he looked up at the fluffy white clouds drifting across the sky, Elmer heard the rumble of a car approaching the house. He rolled onto his belly and watched the apple-red sedan wind down the path and come to a stop near the fenced-in yard. Soon Ron came out into the sun, lifting his hand in greeting, a wide grin on his face. "You must be the Cruz family," he said.

The man behind the wheel opened his car door and stepped out, nodding his head. As tall as Ron, he had tan skin and a trimmed beard that covered his cheeks and chin, but didn't hide his bright smile.

"We are," the man answered, shaking Ron's hand. "I'm Reggie, and this is my wife, Sergeant Cruz." He gestured toward a woman in a green-and-tan army uniform coming around the front of the car. Her jet-black hair was pulled into a tight bun, and she had warm hazel eyes and deep dimples when she smiled.

"You can call me Marisol," she said. "And this is our son, Benicio. . . ." She looked behind her to find no one there. She sighed. "Benny, come on out and say hello."

That's when Elmer noticed the young boy sitting in the back seat of the car with his nose pressed up against the window. His dark, wavy hair stuck out in all different directions, and behind his glasses his wide eyes were almost the same brown as Elmer's paws. He was nervously biting the corner of his lip as he finally pushed open his door and climbed out of the car. "Hi," he mumbled quietly, and waved before shoving his hands back into his pockets.

"Hello there," Ron said. Then he turned to Marisol and whispered, "He isn't scared of dogs, is he?"

Marisol shook her head. "No, he's actually really excited to be here. He's just a little shy with new people. It's one of the reasons we want to adopt a dog. Reggie and I are used to moving every few years, whenever the military reassigns me. But I'm afraid it's been kind of tough on Benny."

"We thought maybe if he had someone to keep him company, that might help," Reggie added. "And nothing makes it easier to meet new friends than a cute puppy, am I right?"

"I can't argue with you there," Ron answered. "Why don't you come inside so you can fill out some paperwork. And Benny?" he said, looking down at the boy, who had nestled against his mom's hip. "If you want, you can stay here and watch the dogs play. It might help you decide what kind you'd like. Just stay outside the gate, all right?"

"I'll keep an eye on him," said Laura, one of the staff members, as she tossed a few more toys into the yard.

After Benny glanced at his mom and dad to make sure it was okay, he grinned and ran right up to the enclosure, peering through the fence.

Elmer couldn't explain why—maybe it was the excited look on the boy's face, or the fact that Benny seemed to need someone just as much as he did—but Elmer wanted this family to adopt him even more than he wanted a chew toy filled with peanut butter. And that was saying a lot!

Elmer trotted over and lifted his front paws onto the fence, letting out a series of yips that meant *Hi! I'm Elmer. Want to play?*

Benny did look down at him, and even stuck his fingers through the fence to boop the tip of his nose. But it wasn't long before his eyes wandered to the side of Elmer's face where his taffy pink tongue poked through. Elmer's wounds had healed, but he knew some people thought he wasn't as cute as the other dogs, and he wasn't as young as the puppies. In human years, he was only ten years old, but in dog years, he was seventy, a senior. So, it came as no surprise that Benny's eyes lit up when Huey, Dewey, and Louie came barreling toward the gate. The boy didn't even notice when Elmer offered him his paw to shake or when he bounced around in a circle, letting his ears flap like bird wings. *He wants a cute little puppy,* Elmer thought. His tail drooped.

Just then, the door of the house opened, and Ron led Reggie and Marisol outside.

"Well, Benny?" Marisol said as she joined her son by the gate. "See any dogs you like?"

Benny nodded and pointed at the German shepherd pups.

"Good choice," Ron said. "German shepherds are great with kids. These are already spoken for, but we do have a new litter that just arrived a few weeks ago. They still need to pass a few medical checks, but I can add you to the adoption waitlist."

"Thanks," said Reggie, resting his hand on Benny's shoulder. "We'll look forward to hearing from you."

With that, the family climbed back into the red car and drove away.

Elmer watched as the Cruz family sped down the road, and Benny turned in his seat to stare out the rear window and smile. For just a moment, Elmer let himself believe that Benny was smiling at him.

Chapter 2

THE NEXT WEEK went by slowly for Elmer. He still loved waking up to breakfast, cuddling with Danny, and running around the yard as fast as his legs could carry him. But he couldn't get Benny and his parents out of his mind. He remembered the salty scent of Benny's hand, Marisol's dimpled smile, and Reggie's deep voice. All those things put together felt like home. Maybe he had given up too soon. He promised himself that if he ever saw them again, he would show them why even if he wasn't perfect, he would be perfect for them.

Every day he practiced being on his best behavior. He sat still for bath time, and instead of shaking the water out of his coat and splashing the groomers, he waited patiently while they towel dried and brushed him. He helped Buster find the chew toy he'd hidden behind a bush. He even secretly practiced a few tricks he'd seen horses perform when Danny and Ron took him to shows. But as the days passed, Elmer started to worry that the Cruzes would never come back.

Then one morning he heard a familiar rumble coming down the road. A few minutes later the doorbell rang, and when Danny opened the door, Elmer saw Marisol and Reggie standing on the other side. *They're here!* Elmer thought. He couldn't hold back his excitement! He let out a few loud barks and galloped toward the door, his nails tapping against the stone floor as he ran. By the time he remembered he was supposed to be on his best behavior, it was too late. He had scrambled right into Marisol's legs.

"Oof!" she cried, stumbling back a little. Then she looked down and saw Elmer gazing up adoringly at her, his tongue lolling to the side as he panted. "Well, who do we have here?"

"Sorry about that," Danny said with a chuckle. "Elmer loves visitors."

Danny scooped Elmer up into his arms, cradling him like a newborn baby.

"He's awfully cute," Reggie said, reaching

out to let Elmer sniff his hand. When Elmer responded with a sideways lick and more happy panting, Reggie rubbed Elmer's belly. "But if you don't mind me asking, what happened to him?" He gestured toward the gap between Elmer's lips.

Ron came out of the kitchen then and said, "It's a long story."

Marisol and Reggie glanced at each other, then Marisol said, "We've got time."

Danny and Ron took turns telling the couple all about how Elmer had been rescued from a bad home and taken to a shelter. He had just about run out of time when one of Danny and Ron's volunteers brought the sad case to their attention. Elmer needed more help than the shelter could give, and the staff there didn't think he would make it.

"Pobrecito," said Marisol, her eyes filled with sympathy. "Poor little thing."

Ron nodded. "He's been through a lot, but he's a fighter."

He told them how they couldn't bear to leave Elmer at the shelter, so they'd brought him to the rescue and got him the medical care he needed. "And he's been here ever since, getting better every day," Danny finished. "He's our little miracle dog."

Ron pulled his hand through his silver hair. "We could talk your ear off about Elmer for hours, but the puppy you came to see is right this way." He motioned for Reggie and Marisol to follow him down the hallway to the back room where they kept the younger puppies.

When Elmer let out a quiet whine, Danny

rocked him in his arms and said, "Now, now . . . Your turn will come soon enough. In the mean- time, how about a little exercise?"

He carried Elmer to the backyard and set him on the ground.

At first Elmer didn't have the heart to run and play. He was too busy thinking about the Cruzes, wondering which of the new pup- pies they would take home instead of him. He half-heartedly chewed on dew-covered blades of grass and lay down, resting his head on his paws. But as he watched the other dogs play, he couldn't help joining in. He still felt disap- pointed, but in his heart, he was a happy dog. Before long, he found himself racing against Joey and practicing his horse tricks. He couldn't jump over a big wooden fence, but he could hop over a pile of twigs.

He pushed off with his back legs, reaching his front paws out in front of him. The first time, he landed right in the middle of the twigs, scattering them with his tail. He nudged them back together and tried again. That time he made it—except for his left back paw. Then he figured out what he was doing wrong. He'd forgotten to account for the length of his body! He needed to get a running start. He circled around and backed far away. Then he dug in his paws and took off like a shot. This time when he jumped,

he felt the air whistle past his ears as he floated above the ground. When he cleared the pile of twigs, he pranced just like his horse friends did. He puffed out his chest and lifted his head proudly. It was then that he heard the applause.

He looked up to see Reggie and Marisol standing in the doorway with Ron and Danny.

"Good job, little guy!" Marisol said, clapping.

"Did you know he could do that?" Reggie

asked Ron and Danny, who both looked pleased, but not all that surprised.

Ron shook his head. "No, but that's Elmer for you. He never gives up."

At the sound of his name, Elmer came running over. Reggie squatted down and Elmer launched himself right into his arms, showering him with his special sideways kisses. Reggie laughed. "I think he likes me."

Marisol gripped her husband's shoulder. "Honey, I know Benny wants a puppy, but . . ."

Reggie nodded knowingly. "But maybe what he needs is an old dog willing to learn new tricks?"

"Exactly." Marisol smiled. Then she turned toward Ron and Danny. "Would it be all right if we took Elmer home with us instead?"

Ron glanced at Elmer, who was still wiggling in Reggie's arms, pressing his wet nose against his neck. He sighed. "I think Elmer would love that. But he is a dog who needs special care and lots of one-on-one time. Are you sure your family is ready for the challenge?"

Marisol stood at attention, her shoulders back and her eyes full of determination. "Sir, yes, sir!" she said. "The Cruz family, reporting for duty."

Ron grinned and said, "All right. Then let's get started, Sergeant."

About an hour later, the trunk of the red car was filled with supplies: a small crate, cans of dog food, medications, a new chew toy that looked like a purple elephant, and a soft blanket. The only thing left to pack was Elmer.

As Danny fit a harness over Elmer's slim body and clipped a navy-blue leash to the ring on top, he whispered, "Well, this is it, boy. You're getting your forever home at last. But remember, you're welcome here any time. Don't forget us, okay?"

Elmer barked and wagged his tail, which meant a lot of things, like: *I won't forget you,* and *I love you.*

But most of all: *Thank you.*

After taking Elmer on a quick walk around the grounds so he could say goodbye to the other dogs and horses, Danny brought him to the car and handed his leash to Reggie. "He's all yours," Danny said. "Take good care of him."

"We will," Reggie answered. "We promise."

He settled Elmer into the back seat, and

Ron and Danny stood in the driveway, waving and smiling at the unique little dachshund. He would miss them, and all the dogs and staff at the rescue. But he couldn't believe his dream to be part of a family was finally coming true.

Reggie and Marisol sat up front and fastened their seat belts, and soon they were rumbling down the road, away from Danny & Ron's Rescue and toward a new life.

Chapter 3

EVEN THOUGH ELMER was excited in the most tail-wagging of ways, the steady motion of the car still rocked him off to sleep. He had almost caught up to the squirrel he was chasing in his dreams when the car came to a stop and Marisol called out, "We're home!"

Elmer eased open his eyes as Reggie lifted him out of the back seat and gently set him down onto the cement driveway. Before him was a stone path lined with pink and red flowers, leading to a sky-blue one-story home, with white shutters and a dark wood door. On the small porch was a love seat swing just wide enough for two people—or one person and a very grateful dachshund. It would give him a great view of the park across the street. Elmer loved the cottage immediately.

"What do you think, boy?" asked Reggie.

In reply, Elmer pranced in happy circles, letting his ears flip and flop as he wound around Reggie's legs.

"Whoa there!" Marisol called with a giggle. "You're getting my husband all tied up." She quickly unraveled the leash that had wrapped around Reggie's legs. Then she bent down to nuzzle Elmer's snout. "You're going to be a little handful, aren't you?"

"Yip!" Elmer replied.

With that, Reggie grabbed a few things from the car, and they headed into the house.

Inside was just as warm and cozy as the outside, though not quite as neat. In the center of the living room was a stack of cardboard boxes marked with words like KITCHEN and BOOKS in black Sharpie. There were more open boxes filled with balled-up newspaper on the kitchen counter, and a few empty boxes were on the floor, tipped over onto their sides. A pair of sneakers with its laces untied lay in a jumble by the couch, and on the coffee table there were scattered crayons and pieces of paper with drawings of puppies on them.

"You'll have to excuse the mess," Reggie said, bending down to unclip Elmer's leash as he sat back on his haunches. "We haven't quite finished unpacking yet."

"But we'll get this place in military shape in no time," added Marisol.

"Oh, you're home!" someone said. A teen-age girl in jeans and sneakers came out from a back room, holding a half-eaten apple.

"Yes," answered Reggie. "Thanks for babysitting, Amanda. I hope Benny wasn't too much trouble."

"No trouble at all. He's in his room reading. All he's been able to talk about is the new puppy. He's studying how to house-train them right now." Amanda crinkled her brow then looked around. "Speaking of the puppy . . . where is it? I thought you were bringing one home with you."

Only then did Marisol and Reggie notice that Elmer was no longer sitting quietly by their side.

"Hey, where did he go?" Reggie asked.

"Elmer?" Marisol called out. "Where are you, boy?"

Elmer could hear Marisol, Reggie, and Amanda whistling, making kissy noises, and repeating his name as they checked behind the TV stand and under the pillows on the couch. He knew he should answer, but he was much too busy settling in to one of the empty boxes near the window. Even though he was excited to be with the Cruz family, he felt nervous, too. He'd lived at the rescue for a long time and knew every inch by heart. Here, everything was

different, with all new sights and smells, but the dark, quiet space inside the box reminded him of his crate back in Dan and Ron's kitchen. He had just settled his snout onto his paws as he curled up against the cardboard wall when one of the box flaps lifted and he saw Marisol's relieved face peek inside.

"There you are," she said, reaching into the

box and sliding her hand under his belly. She pulled him out gently and held him close as she stood. When Elmer whined, sad to see his cardboard crate getting farther and farther away, Marisol stroked his back and cooed into his ear. "Shh . . . it's okay, sweetie."

"Is he all right?" asked Reggie, sounding concerned.

Marisol nodded. "I think he's just a little overwhelmed. I'm sure he's gotten used to his routines and this is a big change for a dog his age. It's a lot to take in."

Grateful that she understood, Elmer tilted his head to one side and licked the tip of her nose. When she smiled and kissed his head, Elmer relaxed. He knew then that everything would be all right.

"So this is the new member of the Cruz family," Amanda said with a squeal. She ran her hand over his back, adding, "Benny's going to looove you!"

"I hope so," said Marisol. "He's not quite the puppy Benny was expecting, but we think he's perfect."

After they paid Amanda and thanked her again for watching their son, Marisol and Reggie made their way to Benny's room. Reggie cradled Elmer in his arms, just as Danny had done back at the dog rescue. But this time, Elmer was too excited to sit still. He squirmed and wriggled impatiently while Marisol knocked on the closed door.

"Benicio? Can we come in? We have a little

canine friend we'd like you to meet," she said, amusement twinkling in her eyes.

There was a brief pause, and then a voice crying, "Come in! Come in!" from inside the room.

Quickly, Marisol turned the doorknob and swung open the door.

By then, Elmer could no longer contain himself. The second he was set onto his paws, he tore across the wood floor to the bed against the wall, where Benny was lying on his stomach with a book open in front of him. Elmer lifted himself up so that his front paws thumped against the mattress. Even standing on his paws, Elmer could barely see over the top of the bed. But soon Benny's wavy brown hair and curious eyes came into view as he leaned over to peer at

the dog. Elmer watched as the excitement that had lit up Benny's face at first slowly turned to confusion and finally disappointment.

"But . . . but . . . where's the German shepherd puppy?"

Marisol and Reggie exchanged a worried glance. "Well . . . we were going to pick up a puppy," Reggie began.

"But then we met Elmer," continued Marisol, "and he just had so much heart and determination. Plus, we think he could really use a friend. Do you think you could be that for him?"

Benny glanced at Elmer again. "I guess so," he said finally. Benny sat up so he could reach down and pet Elmer's head, but Elmer could tell the young boy wasn't sure if he really wanted to be his friend or not.

Elmer wasn't discouraged, though. He'd done a lot of tough things no one thought he could do. And now he vowed to do one more: show the family of his dreams that he could be the dog of theirs.

Chapter 4

ELMER DIDN'T KNOW how to tell time, but he knew it moved extra slow when he was waiting for Benny to come home from school. Whenever any car passed, Elmer perked up, hoping it was the school bus and Benny would appear.

After the fifth car zoomed by, Reggie chuckled beside Elmer and said, "Not yet, buddy.

Relax." He settled the dachshund back into his seat and gave his ear a scratch.

They were sitting together on the porch swing, enjoying the sunshine and afternoon breeze. Elmer had been part of the family for only a couple of weeks, but already he and Reggie had a routine going—breakfast and medicine, nap, walk, nap, play time, nap—and this was his favorite part: school bus watch. As a writer, Reggie had to spend a lot of time working on his book, but when he finished for the day, he and Elmer would sit out on the porch swing and wait for Benny. Elmer loved cuddling with Reggie— especially since every now and then he fed him a delicious treat. But his mind was never far from the boy and how he planned to become Benny's very best friend.

Now that he felt more at home here than when he'd first arrived and had hidden in the cardboard box, he could put all his energy toward being the Cruz family's dream dog. He'd decided that for starters, he would be the first one to greet Benny as soon as he stepped off the bus, and then they'd have fun, fun, fun together. They could play in the backyard, and Benny was sure to be impressed once he saw how fast Elmer could run!

At last, a long yellow school bus pulled up near the house and came to a stop. The doors slid open with a *ksshh* sound and Benny plodded down the steps and onto the sidewalk. He gave the bus driver a half-hearted wave when she wished him a good day before closing the door, but he never lifted his eyes from the ground. He looked sad. *I can fix that!* thought Elmer.

He glanced at Reggie, who grinned as he set him onto the floor and said, "Okay, go on."

Quickly, Elmer hurried down the ramp that Marisol had placed over the stairs. Because of his long back and short legs, sometimes stairs were tough to handle, but the ramp made it easier. He met Benny on the walkway, just inside the gate, and circled him three times, yipping all the while. *Hi, Benny! I'm so happy to see you! Want to play?*

But Benny wasn't in the mood. He stopped to pat Elmer on the head, then kept walking.

Reggie stood at the top of the stairs with his arms open wide. When Benny reached him, he pulled the boy into a hug. "How was school today, Benicio?" he asked.

"Fine," Benny grunted.

"Are you sure? It doesn't sound like it was fine."

Benny shrugged but fell silent. Then after a pause, he said, "I don't want to talk about it."

Reggie peered at his son, his eyes darkening with concern. "Well, all right. But I hope you know I'm here whenever you're ready to talk."

"I know. Thanks, Dad," Benny said quietly.

"You know what?" Reggie rested his hands on Benny's shoulders. "I could use some help with Elmer. Why don't you give me a hand?"

A few minutes later, Benny and his father were cross-legged on the floor of the living room, with Elmer sitting between them. Reggie held up a double-sided stainless-steel comb with a light purple handle.

"Elmer has long hair, and it can tangle easily. It's important to comb it out once in a while so it doesn't get matted," he said, handing the comb to Benny. Elmer looked from the comb to the boy and whined softly. He'd never let anyone besides Ron and Danny and their groomers comb him before. Plus, this wasn't part of the plan. He'd wanted to show Benny how fun and fast he could be, not how much he could shed. But then he reminded himself that part of being a family's dream dog was letting them take care of him. They seemed to like making sure he had enough to eat and a warm place to sleep. So maybe Benny would have fun combing his hair. He let out a few nervous pants then tried to calm down.

"I don't know, Dad. He looks kind of scared."

"I think he's just excited," Reggie assured him. "He's been waiting for you all day. But just in case, talk to him. Let him know you don't mean him any harm."

Benny put the comb down then reached out and stroked Elmer's back. "It's okay, Elmer. I promise I'm not going to hurt you. I just need to untangle your hair, okay?"

The soft tone of Benny's voice and the understanding look in his eyes was so soothing that Elmer flopped on his side and thumped his tail against the floor. Benny gasped as he glanced at his father in amazement. "It worked!"

Reggie grinned back at him. "Told you so. You're a natural." As Benny began to gently comb through Elmer's hair, Reggie stood up. "While you're doing that, I'll go make you a snack. In the meantime, keep talking to Elmer. It might make you feel better."

Benny sighed as he watched his father walk toward the kitchen. "He doesn't get it," he whispered. "It's so hard being the new kid every few months. Nobody would even sit with me at lunch."

Picking up on the sad shift in Benny's voice, Elmer lifted himself up enough to stare at Benny, who stared right back at him.

"I bet you think I'm making it sound worse than it is, but I'm not. At recess, Kyle and A. J. picked teams for baseball, and no one asked me to play. I know I'm quiet, but it's like they don't even see me." Benny stopped to remove some hair from the comb and toss it in the wastepaper basket. But Elmer thought he heard a little hitch in his throat, like the sad sound Elmer sometimes made when Marisol left for work at the base in the morning. Is that how Benny felt while he was at school?

"The worst part is," said Benny, "I think Kyle and A. J. are pretty cool. If I could just get their attention—impress them somehow—maybe they'd want to be my friend. Then everyone else would too."

When Benny stopped combing for a second, Elmer saw his chance to get up and give Benny's face a lick. He thumped his paws against the boy's chest and nuzzled his neck, then poked his wet nose into Benny's ear. It was a flurry of doggy love meant to say, *I'm already your friend!*

Benny laughed as he tried, without much success, to get the energetic dachshund under control. "Okay, okay . . . I get it! You like me. Can I finish combing your hair now?"

It took a minute, but eventually Benny was able to coax Elmer onto his other side so that he could comb the rest of the dog's hair and his bushy tail. When he was done, Elmer's coat was shiny and tangle free.

"You know what?" Benny said. "I do feel a little better. You're a pretty good listener, Elmer."

Those were the last words Elmer heard before he drifted off to sleep, thinking happy thoughts about how he had been a very good boy today. He'd gotten closer to Benny just by being himself. With any luck, he would soon be the best friend Benny needed, and Benny would be his, too.

Chapter 5

LATER THAT NIGHT, after the whole family had eaten dinner and Benny had gone off to bed, Elmer curled up in his crate, listening to Marisol and Reggie talk as they sat together on the couch. Marisol told Reggie about her day at work, then Reggie described the pages he had written for his book. But soon they mentioned Benny, and Elmer's ears perked up.

"I overheard him talking to Elmer earlier," Reggie said. "It sounds like he's still having a hard time making friends at school. I'm worried about him."

"Me too," Marisol agreed. "I was hoping that having a new dog to talk about would help him break the ice."

Reggie nodded. "It probably would if he wasn't too shy to talk to the kids in the first place."

"Hm . . . you have a point," said Marisol.

"You mean I'm right?" Reggie smiled as he slid one arm around Marisol's shoulders. "So this is what it feels like!"

Marisol giggled and poked him in the side with her finger. "Don't let it get to your head."

Reggie gave her forehead a kiss. "All right,

Sergeant. Do you have any idea what we should do?"

"I might," she said, sounding hopeful. "Do you remember how Elmer jumped over that pile of twigs the day we first met him?"

"Of course," said Reggie. "It's almost like he was putting on a show for us. Sometimes it still feels that way. For an older dog, he has a lot of energy."

"Exactly! Well, when Lieutenant Vega adopted his dog, Ginger, she was energetic too—so much so that he thought agility classes might be good for her. There's a four-week youth dog-training program downtown. He enrolled Ginger and his daughter, Cathy, and it ended up being great for both of them. Ginger learned some useful skills, and his daughter made a lot of friends. She looked forward to going after school, and the course even ended in a doggy talent show."

"And you think that course could help Benny and Elmer?" Reggie asked.

Marisol glanced toward the crate, where Elmer was gnawing on a stuffed giraffe.

"It couldn't hurt," she said. "If it works, Benny will already have dogs in common with the kids he meets. Training them together will give them something to talk about."

Reggie lifted his eyebrows, as if he was impressed. "True. And maybe Elmer can use up some of his energy."

"We can dream!" Marisol said with a grin.

They decided to enroll Benny and Elmer in the dog-training program first thing in the morning. And just before they turned off all the lights and went to bed, Marisol peeked into Elmer's crate and whispered, "Good night, little guy. Get plenty of rest now. Pretty soon, you're going to school!"

That Saturday, Elmer trotted next to Benny into the best place on earth.

At least, that's what the dog-training grounds looked like to him. It was a huge indoor gym, but the floor was covered in green felt, and everywhere Elmer looked, there were things for him to play with. On one side were colorful ramps in three different sizes, and long vinyl tubes big enough to run through sat like giant blue and yellow snakes near the back. In the center of the floor were several poles all in

a row, a thin tire hanging between two stands, and more sticks set up at different heights. They were almost like what Danny and Ron taught the horses to jump over in their shows! Elmer wondered if he would get to jump over the sticks too. He hoped so!

But the best part was that he wasn't the only dog there. Four other kids and their dogs were already milling around inside, waiting for the instructors to finish talking to their parents. One of the kids waved.

She was a young girl around Benny's age. Her green eyes looked big behind her glasses, which had yellow-and-blue glittery frames that matched her tie-dyed T-shirt. Benny seemed surprised.

"Is she a friend of yours?" Marisol asked.

"She goes to my school," Benny answered slowly. "But she's never talked to me before."

Reggie gave him a gentle nudge and said, "Look at that. You're making friends already. Go on, Son. Say hi. We'll be right here waiting for you when the class is over."

Benny hesitated. Elmer could tell the boy was nervous, but maybe he just needed some help from his new best friend. Elmer tugged on his leash, leaving Benny no choice but to walk toward the girl. As they drew closer, Elmer started pulling against his harness for two reasons: to help Benny overcome his shyness, and to meet the waving girl's dog, who pulled against her harness too. She was a medium-size pup with a light brown coat and golden eyes. She seemed to be smiling at him.

"Is she friendly?" Benny asked. Benny's parents had taught him that it's always a good idea to ask the owner if it's safe to come near their dog.

"Very," she said with an exaggerated eye roll. "Coda would be the worst guard dog in the whole world because she loves everyone."

Benny let out a small laugh and nodded. "Mine is the same way. Especially if you've got"—he lowered his voice to a whisper— "t-r-e-a-t-s."

The girl laughed in goofy-sounding hiccups. When they finally stopped, she held out her hand for Benny to shake. "I'm Kitts," she said, and Elmer noticed she had at least ten colorful friendship bracelets on each wrist, matching the ties wrapped around her braids.

"I'm Benny, and this is my dog, Elmer." He jutted his chin toward Elmer and smiled. Elmer loved it when he did that. He sat back on his haunches and wagged his tail until Benny rewarded him with a head scratch. Then he went back to sniffing Coda, who smelled like doggy shampoo and wildflowers.

"I've seen you around school," said Kitts. "You're new, right?"

Benny nodded. "We just moved here a little while ago. I don't really know too many people yet." Elmer heard a tiny bit of sadness creep back into Benny's voice.

But Kitts gave him a sunny smile and said, "Well, now you know me! And Coda. How long have you had your dog?"

"Just a couple of weeks. My parents adopted

him from a place called Danny & Ron's Rescue."

Suddenly, Kitts's eyes lit up even more. "That's where we found Coda!"

"Really?"

"Really!" She bent down to ruffle her dog's coat. "Aren't Danny and Ron the best? If it wasn't for them, Coda might still be at the shelter. When they took her in, she had a bad ear infection and heartworm, so no one wanted to adopt her. Can you imagine not giving a sweet dog like her a home just because she had some health problems?"

"I don't know," Benny said with a shrug. "That kind of thing can be a lot to deal with for some people."

"That's true. I just think everybody deserves a chance—especially dogs."

Elmer happily accepted Kitts's scratch behind his ear.

Benny chewed on one end of his lip. "Elmer had a lot of health problems too. You probably think he looks a little . . . weird."

"Hm." Kitts stood up and gazed at Elmer. He knew she was looking at his sideways tongue and floppy ears, but she didn't seem bothered by them. "Not at all," she said finally. "He's super

cute in his own special way. Besides, what's so bad about being different?"

Elmer liked Kitts immediately. And he liked the smile spreading over Benny's face even more.

Finally, the instructors—Jeremy Eng, and Paige and Persephone Ellingston—were ready for the class to begin.

By then, Elmer and Coda had finished their sniffy greetings and were lying down beside each other, panting happily. They had decided to be friends. And it seemed like their owners had too.

Chapter 6

THE FIRST DOG-TRAINING class wasn't Elmer's finest moment—at least not if the goal was to finish the course.

Jeremy had started with the simple stuff: making sure the dogs knew how to sit, stay, and come when called. Elmer wasn't bad at those things thanks to his time at the dog rescue. But he got a little confused when it came to the obstacles. Paige had shown Benny how to lead Elmer up one half of the A-frame ramp and down the other, but right at the top, Elmer got distracted by a barking French bulldog and ran back the way he came. The vinyl tunnel didn't go much better. Benny led Elmer into the opening, but once he got inside, he kind of forgot why he was running. The center of the tunnel glowed with a warm light, and it seemed like the perfect place to lie down and clean his paws. When Persephone called his name, he stood up and padded out a little bit farther to see what she wanted. Only when she held out her hand, which she had filled with treats, did Elmer leave the pretty tunnel behind. But he felt ashamed when he spotted Benny shaking his head at him. Oh no. Had he let Benny down?

He'd been trying so hard to prove to him that he was the best dog he could possibly have. But so far he hadn't even shown Benny he was the best dog in the gym. Maybe the tunnel hadn't been a good place to clean his paws after all.

When they stopped for a water break, Benny slumped against the wall next to Kitts, then slid all the way down onto the floor. "It's no use!" he complained. "We've been at this for an hour already, and Elmer hasn't even made it through the tunnel yet."

"Big deal!" said Kitts, sitting beside him. "It's his first time. He'll get it eventually."

"Easy for you to say," Benny answered. "You and Coda are an awesome team! She listens to everything you say."

Kitts smiled. "That's only because I've had

Coda a lot longer than you've had Elmer. He has to practice, that's all."

"But what if we don't get any better? We have to perform in the talent show at the end of the course. If we mess up, it'll be so embarrassing!" Benny chewed his lip nervously.

Kitts shook her head at Benny. "Don't worry about that," she suggested. "For now, just have fun. Maybe it would help if Elmer had a friend show him how it's done. Come on. Let's run through the course together." She stood up and tugged on Coda's leash, then gestured for Benny and Elmer to follow.

Kitts had a lot of great ideas, but this was her best one yet as far as Elmer was concerned. Determined to show Benny how well he could complete any challenge in his path, he tuned out all the other dogs and noises and focused on Coda. With her running ahead, Elmer made it up the ramp and down the other side, and he didn't get distracted in the middle of the tunnel, because he was following Coda through it. They even tried the bar jumps, and this time Elmer led the way when Coda seemed nervous.

Elmer ran and leaped over the bar as if it was only a pile of twigs on the ground.

"Good boy!" Benny shouted, waiting for Elmer to sit before giving him a treat. But Elmer didn't even need the small dog biscuit to feel good. Benny's proud smile was enough.

By the end of class, Elmer felt a lot more confident, and Benny seemed happier too.

"Thanks, Kitts," said Benny. "We couldn't have done it without you and Coda."

Kitts flashed a bright smile. "You're welcome. With a little practice, you two will rule this course in no time!" Kitts and Benny high-fived.

Before Elmer knew it, they were back home. But he couldn't stop thinking about his new friend, Coda, or how much fun it was to run through the obstacle course with Benny. He guessed Benny felt the same way, because over the next couple of weeks, he used items from his room to run drills with Elmer in their back-yard. He didn't have poles that stuck into the ground, but he did have plastic bowling pins. And he didn't have a low wall for Elmer to jump over, but he did have stacks of books.

When Elmer had mastered that makeshift obstacle course, Benny took Elmer to the park across the street and let him practice jumping over fallen tree trunks. After one particularly good jump, Elmer heard a boy say, "Cool!"

Benny whirled around, and Elmer heard his breath catch. He didn't know why the boy cruising toward them on a sleek black skate-board covered in stickers seemed to make Benny nervous, but he did. His light hair hung over his eyes a little, and he had on a plain white T-shirt. He wasn't smiling, but he wasn't frowning, either. The kid seemed friendly enough to Elmer, but he moved in close to Benny, ready to protect him just in case.

"Er, hi, A. J.," said Benny awkwardly.

"Hey," the boy answered. He pointed at him with his index finger. "Benny, right?"

Benny nodded.

"I didn't know you had a dog that could do tricks."

This time Benny beamed. "He just started learning how, but he's getting pretty good. He's fast, too. I'll bet he's even faster than your skateboard."

A. J. laughed and pointed at Elmer. "That dog? Doubt it. But maybe we can have a race sometime."

Elmer didn't like it that A. J. didn't believe Benny about how fast he could run. And he really didn't like the way A. J. smirked at him. But Benny didn't seem to notice.

"Sure, whenever you want!" Benny said.

A. J. flipped his skateboard up into his hand, and kneeled down to face Elmer. "Get ready to lose, little guy." He reached out to pet Elmer's head, but Elmer backed away. "Aw, scared of a little competition, huh?" A. J. taunted, sticking his tongue out at him. "Whatever. See you at school, Benny."

"See ya," he answered. Elmer could tell Benny was happy about his new friend. But Elmer wasn't sure that he was.

Chapter 7

FOR THE NEXT few days, Benny spent lots of time with Elmer, running with him in the backyard or playing fetch. At first Elmer loved it. Nothing made him happier than chasing after a rubber ball and bringing it back to Benny. But he couldn't figure out why the boy seemed a little sadder each day—not until Benny talked to him about it one night as he gave Elmer a bath.

"I don't get it," Benny complained while he crouched in the tub beside Elmer and massaged doggy shampoo into his wet coat. "A. J. seemed so impressed when he saw you doing tricks in the park. I guess I was wrong, but I thought he wanted to be my friend."

Elmer let out a huff that meant *Friends don't tease your dog.* But Benny must have heard *Please don't get shampoo in my eyes.*

"Don't worry, I'll be careful," Benny said, gently tilting Elmer's head back so that the warm spray of water washed the soap down past his ears and into the tub. Then he aimed the nozzle at Elmer's paws and sprayed until all the suds had swirled down the drain. Elmer didn't like getting bathed, but with Benny it wasn't so bad.

When he was done, Benny reached for a towel, wrapped it around Elmer, and lifted him out of the tub. While he dried Elmer's hair, he let out a deep sigh. "At school, A. J. acts like he doesn't even know me," he said. "His friends do too. When I try to talk to them, they just ask me to move out of their way or ask me for the

answer to a math problem. I don't think they'll ever let me into their group."

Elmer couldn't understand anyone not wanting to be Benny's friend. He was Elmer's favorite person in the whole world . . . until he brought out the eye drops, that is. At the first sign of the little bottle, Elmer whined and turned his head away.

"Aw, come on, buddy. You know I have to give you the drops to make sure your eye doesn't get infected. I promise it won't hurt at all."

Elmer shook out his coat, spraying water everywhere. Benny held up his hands and squeezed his eyes shut, but he still got soaked. "Hey!" he cried. "This is supposed to be your bath time, not mine!"

Maybe now he'll forget about the drops and go change his clothes instead, thought Elmer. But when Benny eased his eyes open again, he wagged a finger at Elmer. "Nice try, but that's not going to stop me from giving you the medicine you need."

Elmer tried making Benny chase him around the small bathroom, but in the end, Benny captured and held him gently until he calmed down. Then he opened Elmer's injured eye with two fingers and moved the dropper over it. With a tap, a few drops slid in. He had to admit that Benny was right—it didn't hurt.

"See? That wasn't so bad, was it?"

Elmer gave him a sideways lick and his best smile.

Benny cradled Elmer's face in his hands and smiled back. "I may not have friends at school, but I'm glad I have you."

Me too, thought Elmer. Benny gave him a quick hug, then reached for another towel to dry himself off.

"Everything okay in here?" Reggie asked, peeking his head into the bathroom.

"Yeah," Benny answered, his voice muffled by the towel. "Elmer just turned his body into a sprinkler." The two of them laughed, and for a while, everything seemed just fine.

But the next day, when Benny got off the school bus, instead of his usual blue mood, he looked happy, excited even—which wasn't usual for him at all.

"It happened!" Benny gushed to Elmer and

his dad as he greeted them on the porch. "A. J. and Kyle invited me to hang out with them and their friends in the park later!"

Reggie looked surprised. Benny had told him all about how A. J. and Kyle ignored him at school. "What changed?" he asked.

Benny shrugged. "I don't know. At lunch, they were talking about Kyle's new iguana, and I said I had a rescue dog, and I guess that reminded A. J. that he met Elmer once, and he wanted to see some of the tricks he's learned in the training classes. Can I go, Dad? Pleeease?"

Reggie gave Benny a big smile. "Of course," he said. "But on three conditions: One, you have to finish your homework first. Two, make sure you clean up after Elmer in the park. And three, be home by dinnertime."

"Done!" cried Benny. With that, he hurried off to his room, pulled his notebook out of his backpack, and got to work. When he finished, he gave Elmer's coat a quick brush and slid on his harness. Then he grabbed a small baggie full of Elmer's favorite treats and a water bottle in case he got thirsty. "Okay, boy, are you ready to go to the park?" he asked.

Elmer barked twice, nice and loud, which meant *Yes! Let's go!*

Benny and Elmer found the kids just where A. J. said they would be—near the playground. A. J. was on his skateboard, kicking off with one foot then cruising in smooth circles around the others, who sat at a picnic table near the slides, looking bored. Two girls, Daisy Perez and Renee Jones, were playing a card game. Kyle Scanlon

sat on a silver-colored dirt bike with both feet planted on the ground. And Martin Chung was chewing gum and sketching characters from the latest superhero movie.

When they caught sight of Benny approaching, A. J. gave him a head nod and said, "Hey."

"Hey," Benny said in return. Elmer could tell by the way his voice quivered that he was nervous, even though he was trying not to show it.

"Is this the dog you told us about, A. J.?" asked Martin, closing his sketchbook to stare at Elmer with wonder.

A. J. nodded as he came to a stop and stepped on the tail end of his skateboard so that it stuck up at an angle. "That's the one!" he said as he shook his blond hair out of his face.

For a moment, Benny smiled. "Did he tell

you about the tricks Elmer can do? Because he's been working hard on his jumps and pole weaving. There's going to be a big talent show at the training gym and—"

"Whoa! You were right," Kyle interrupted. "His dog is missing, like, half his face!"

"Ew. Really?" said Daisy.

The other kids laughed as Kyle hopped off of his bike and moved closer. "Awesome!" he said, bending down to look at Elmer.

Quickly, Elmer scooted behind Benny's legs, his tail stiff.

"Stop," Renee said. "I think you're scaring him."

"Yeah, leave him alone," Benny added.

Kyle held up his hands and backed off. "Sorry."

But Benny shifted uncomfortably on his

feet, as if he were worried that he had over-reacted and insulted his new friends. "S-sorry," Benny stammered. "It's just that—"

He never got to finish his sentence because Kyle interrupted with a whisper. "Nobody look up. It's that weird girl from school."

Daisy tsked. "You guys are so *mean*." But she said it with a giggle in her voice, like she thought "mean" might be the same thing as "funny."

"She brings it on herself," Kyle reasoned. "Her clothes have so many colors it hurts my eyes."

"And she is *way* too happy about *every*-thing," A. J. piled on. "Even homework." The others laughed as A. J. went on to do a quiet impression of Kitts begging the teacher to give her more work to do.

But not one of the things they said about

Kitts sounded bad to Elmer. He couldn't understand why they were making fun of her. And he really couldn't understand why Benny wasn't coming to her defense. Elmer peeked out from behind Benny's legs and spotted Kitts, skipping and whistling to herself as she walked Coda through the park. Elmer's tail immediately started wagging, but Benny didn't seem glad to see her at all. In fact, he sort of bent his head and turned away. But not before Kitts had spotted him, too.

She stopped in her tracks, lifted her right arm, and waved it wildly. "Hi, Benny! Hi, Elmer!" she cried.

"You *know* that girl?" A. J. asked Benny, his eyes widening.

"Uh . . . not really," Benny answered. "We just

got our dogs from the same place, that's all."

He fell quiet and waited for Kitts to move on. Seeing the hurt in Kitts's eyes as she pulled Coda away, Elmer felt confused. Why did Benny ignore her and Coda? Weren't *they* his friends? It seemed like Benny had pretended not to know Kitts just because A. J. and the others didn't like her. Did that mean if they decided they didn't like Elmer, Benny would stop being *his* friend too?

Seeming to sense Elmer's discomfort, Benny pulled out the bag of treats and offered some to Elmer. But Elmer didn't feel very hungry. He sniffed at the peanut-butter-flavored snack, then turned his head away and huffed.

"Looks like he's mad at you," A. J. observed.

"Um, I think maybe he's just not feeling

well," Benny said. "I should get him home."

He said goodbye to the other kids and led Elmer out of the park, across the street, and into the house.

At the sound of the door closing, Reggie emerged from the kitchen. "Back so soon?"

"Yeah, I think Elmer's tired," Benny said. He knelt to take off the harness, a moment when Elmer would usually sneak in a few of his signature sideways kisses. But this time he just waited patiently for Benny to slide the harness over his head. "You're just a dog," Benny whispered. "You don't understand." But Elmer understood just fine. He moved past Benny, padded off to his crate, and lay down. If his friendship with Benny depended on whether A. J. liked him or not, then maybe they wouldn't be friends for very long.

Chapter 8

A FEW DAYS LATER, when Benny and Elmer walked into the training gym, Elmer could tell that Benny was feeling anxious. And when he saw Kitts look at Benny and turn away, he knew why. Though Elmer had mostly forgiven Benny—it was hard for a dog to hold a grudge against his humans—Kitts hadn't.

Instead of waiting for Benny and Elmer near

the entrance like she usually did, she had sta-tioned herself on the other side of the gym with Paige, who was teaching Kitts how to guide Coda through the hanging circle that looked like a tire. It was one of the few obstacles that Elmer thought was too high for him to jump through.

Benny hung his head low as he led Elmer over to the weaving poles. He let Jeremy show him how to space the poles far apart at first while Elmer ran between them, then move the poles closer and closer until they were in a straight line and Elmer could dodge back and forth.

"Don't worry if this takes some time to learn," Jeremy said kindly. "It's a little trickier than the others, so we'll have to walk him through it over and over again. But once he gets it right, it's a real crowd pleaser!" He smiled down at Elmer and added, "What do you say, Elmer? Do we have a deal?"

Elmer sat on his haunches and offered Jeremy his paw.

Jeremy laughed. "What a pro!"

For the next twenty minutes, Benny walked Elmer through the poles, letting him get a feel for what they were asking him to do. Each time Elmer did it right, Benny gave him a treat. They took turns switching off with Misty, the husky and terrier mix, who had one blue eye and one brown. Her owner, Matt, seemed nice enough. But Benny was too distracted to make friends. He kept sneaking peeks over at Kitts and Coda, who were having a great time jumping through the circle and *not* looking at Benny.

Finally, Paige announced that class was

over for the day, and they would be contact-
ing each of them soon to talk about the talent
show. Again, Elmer smelled the extra salty scent
of fear coming off Benny's skin.

Then he got a look of determination in his
eyes and said, "Come on, Elmer. One last run."

But instead of running up the ramp or

through the vinyl tunnel, they just jogged long enough to catch up to Kitts. Benny tapped her shoulder and cleared his throat.

"Um, Kitts, can I talk to you for a second?"

Kitts turned around and looked at him with a shocked expression. "What? You mean that you can see me now? I thought I was invisible!"

Benny sighed. He'd had that coming. "I know—that was pretty crummy what I did in the park the other day, pretending I didn't see you."

Kitts folded her arms and pursed her lips. "Yeah, it was. So why did you do it?"

"Um, well, er . . . ," Benny began. "I was hanging out with those kids from school, and I really wanted them to like me."

"And you didn't think they would if you were my friend?" Kitts asked.

Benny took a deep breath and shrugged. "Maybe? They don't usually talk to me, so when A. J. invited me to the park, I was happy. But then we saw you . . . and you were whistling and skipping." Benny swallowed. "They said you were . . ."

"Weird?" Kitts finished for him.

Benny nodded. "I just . . . got scared that they would think I was weird too."

For a moment, Kitts's face fell. Her feelings were clearly hurt. But then she shook her head. "I don't really care what they think of me because they're not very nice. So why do *you* care so much?"

"I don't know," Benny said, looking confused.

Kitts's frown grew deeper. "Well, I know one

thing: I'd rather be weird than be a bad friend," she said. "Come on, Coda."

Elmer barely had time to say goodbye to Coda before Kitts led her away. He whined as he watched them go, and he could swear that he heard Benny groan too.

That evening, Paige called, just as she'd promised, to talk about the talent show. Benny and his family gathered around the kitchen table and turned on the speakerphone. Elmer was curled up on Benny's lap and he could hear the boy's stomach rumbling. But it wasn't a hunger growl; it was the sound Benny's stomach made when he was upset.

"As you know," Paige said to Marisol and Reggie, "each of our students competes in the final talent show. They can either run the whole course or choose a specific skill if they want . . . Whatever the dog and his person are most comfortable doing. So, Benny, what do you think Elmer's talent will be?"

Benny shook his head at his parents and lifted one shoulder. Elmer had gotten pretty good at reading Benny's movements, and that one meant he had no idea. Marisol patted his hand to reassure him, then asked Paige, "What did the other students choose?"

Paige rattled off what the other dogs would be doing. One would be focusing on the bar jumps. One would do the ramps and tunnels. One planned to start with the weaving poles and then tackle the seesaw. Finally she mentioned Coda. "She's a bit of a star," Paige confessed. "She's going to be running the full course."

Benny's parents oohed and aahed. "Bold move," Reggie said, nodding and pushing his mouth into an upside-down *U*.

"Coda must be a pretty special dog," added Marisol.

And suddenly Benny's tan cheeks flushed red and his mouth tightened. "Elmer's a special dog too," he insisted. "Even more special than Coda. He's going to run the full course too, and he'll beat her time."

On the other end of the line, Paige went quiet for a second. She sounded hesitant when she spoke. "Uh . . . are you sure, Benny? I don't think Elmer has quite mastered the weaving poles yet, and he's never even tried the tire jump. You don't want to have him bite off more than he can chew—"

Benny pointed his finger at the phone, as if Paige could see him. "Elmer can chew just fine! The only reason he hasn't tried that other stuff is because he didn't want to make Coda feel bad. You sign us up and we'll be ready," Benny said confidently.

"Okay . . . if you're sure," Paige said. "But you can call me any time before the show to change your mind, all right?"

"I won't," said Benny.

By the time Benny got to his room, he had changed his mind.

"This is terrible!" he ranted to Elmer, who lay on Benny's bed watching the boy pace back and forth. When Benny was upset or anxious it made Elmer feel that way too. He found himself panting as if he had just run around the yard. "Paige was right—you're not ready for the poles, you've never made it through the vinyl tunnel on your own, and the tire stand is too high for you. What are we going to do?"

Elmer had no clue. He would try his best not to let Benny down, but what if his best wasn't good enough? What if he couldn't do some of the tricks? His mind racing, Elmer got up and walked in tight circles on the bed, letting out soft whines.

Finally Benny sat with a *whumpf* beside Elmer, then reached out to hug him. "I'm sorry, boy," he said. "I didn't mean to worry you. We'll find a way to get through this together. . . . I hope."

Just then came a soft knock at the door, and Marisol eased her way into the room. "Mind if I come in?" she asked.

Benny shook his head and shifted Elmer over so they could make room for his mom.

Marisol sat next to him and laced the fingers of her hands together. "So . . . ," she started. "You sounded a little upset back there. Anything you want to talk about?"

Benny groaned. "I've ruined everything! I was really mean to Kitts just to impress some kids at school I don't even like. And now I've made a promise that Elmer and I can't keep, and it's going to be sooo embarrassing." He threw himself into his mother's arms and squeezed her tight.

She patted his back gently. "Ay, Benicio. No te preocupes."

"Don't worry?" he said, his voice strained. "How can I not worry?"

"Ask yourself this instead," Marisol replied. "Will worrying change anything?"

Benny thought quietly for a moment as he pulled back from his mom. "No," he said finally.

"Okay, then." Marisol nodded. "So if worrying won't change anything, what will?"

Benny glanced at Elmer and sighed. "Telling Paige the truth—that Elmer can't do the whole course."

"Good. And what would make things better with your friend?"

"Saying I'm sorry?" Benny asked. "For real this time?"

Marisol's dimples deepened as she smiled at her son. "That's a good place to start."

Chapter 9

ELMER POUNCED ON the car door again and barked at the window. *We're here! Open the door!* But his humans didn't seem to understand. They'd been parked in front of a beige ranch-style house for ten minutes now, but neither Marisol nor Ben showed any signs of movement.

"I don't think this is the right house," said

Benny. "Kitts always wears at least ten colors, and this house only has one or two."

Marisol drummed her fingers against the steering wheel. "You're stalling."

"Who, me? Nuh-uh. No way."

His mother lifted one eyebrow at him and waited. It was her foolproof mom/sergeant move, and Benny was powerless against it. He groaned.

"What if I changed my mind?"

Marisol shook her head. "Sorry, kid. No turning back now. Kitts's parents are already expecting you. Do you think Kitts would like it if you let her parents down?"

Benny breathed out. "No. But what if Kitts doesn't want to talk to me? Or what if she still won't accept my apology?"

Marisol gave him a half grin and blinked

slowly. "That's the chance you take. But just because she might not accept your apology doesn't mean you shouldn't offer it to her anyway, right?"

Benny nodded miserably.

"No matter what happens, you call me, and I'll come pick you up."

Elmer filled the quiet pause that followed with another series of impatient barks. *I smell Coda! Let's go find Coda! Coda, Coda, Coda!*

"All right, all right," Benny said at last. He pushed open his door and climbed out of the car. Then he let Benny out too.

Finally!

"Good luck, Private!" Marisol called. Benny shot his mom his best salute, then pressed the doorbell.

A few minutes later, Kitts's mother led Elmer and Benny to the backyard, where Kitts and Coda were playing tug-of-war with a length of rainbow-colored rope.

Coda! Elmer ran toward his friend, trailing his leash behind him. Coda dropped the rope and met Elmer halfway. The two of them sniffed and circled each other, then rolled around on the grass.

But Benny's approach was shy and slow. "H-hi, Kitts," he said, holding up his hand.

"What are you doing here?" she asked, stepping past the two wrestling dogs.

"I, um . . . I wanted to say that I'm really sorry. You were right. I messed up and was a bad friend. Can you please give me another chance?"

Kitts crossed her arms over her lemon-yellow tank top. "I don't know . . . What do you think, Coda? Should we forgive Benny?"

Right on cue, Coda broke away from Elmer just long enough to press her heavy paws against Benny's legs, requesting hugs and kisses. Benny gave her both.

"So much for playing it cool," Kitts said with a laugh. "Fine. We forgive you."

Benny breathed a sigh of relief. "Thanks. Elmer and I really missed you and Coda."

Kitts tugged on the friendship bracelets on her right wrist. "We missed you and Elmer, too. Especially during dog training. I saw Elmer learning to do the pole weaving move. Is that going to be his talent for the show?"

At the mention of the show, Benny winced and held his stomach, as if he felt sick.

"You're not going to believe the boneheaded thing I did," he said.

"I might. What was it?"

Benny told her all about how Paige had called to ask what Elmer planned to do in the talent show, and he'd blurted out that Elmer would be running the whole course.

"So now I have to call Paige back and tell her

the truth—we're only ready to do a few parts."

"Not necessarily," Kitts said, looking thoughtful.

"What do you mean?" asked Benny.

"Can you and Elmer meet me at the gym after school tomorrow?"

"I think so," Benny answered. "Why?"

Kitts flashed him her brightest smile. "I have an idea."

The next day Elmer padded into the gym with Benny, not sure what to expect. It wasn't their usual day for lessons, but with the talent show coming up, Jeremy and Paige had given Kitts and Benny permission to get in some extra practice.

Kitts and Coda arrived at the same time,

and right away Kitts explained to Benny why they were there. "I know you think that Elmer isn't ready to complete the whole course. But remember how he did when he followed Coda's lead?"

Benny nodded. "That's the only time he's gone through the tunnel without stopping."

"Right!" said Kitts. "And Elmer helped Coda out with the bar jumps. Really, they both do better when they work together."

Benny's mouth gaped a little. "So you think they can train together even if they're going to compete against each other in the show?"

"Why not?" Kitts shrugged. "Helping each other is what friends do, right?"

Benny smiled. "Right."

Kitts pulled a few pieces of kibble out of her

pocket, and said, "Then let's get started!"

For the next hour, Benny and Kitts walked the dogs through the whole routine. Some of the obstacles they did together, like the A-frame ramp, the tunnel, and the low bar jumps. And for some of them they took turns. Coda leaped through the tire jump first, and Elmer wasn't sure he could follow her. But then he remembered how fast he could run and decided to give it a try. To everyone's surprise, he sailed right through the circle and landed smoothly on the other side.

"Great job, Elmer!" Benny said breathlessly as he jogged beside him.

Elmer could tell he had made him proud, which made Elmer feel proud too.

Next they worked on the weaving poles and the long jumps. Each of the dogs made some

mistakes, but Elmer had never had so much fun at the gym.

When they were done, Kitts clapped excitedly. "This will be the best talent show ever!" she cried. Elmer yipped, and Coda barked. But the best part for Elmer was seeing Benny's grateful smile.

Chapter 10

ELMER **WOKE UP** bright and early that Saturday morning. He stretched out his long body and let out a slow yawn. He'd gotten a good night's sleep, but it was time to get going. The day of the talent show had finally arrived.

The night before, Benny had taken the time to brush out Elmer's hair until it was soft and shiny as satin. He'd even cleaned his ears and nails and brushed his teeth. Elmer hadn't even budged when it came time for his eye drops.

This morning, when Reggie let him out of his crate, Elmer found his breakfast waiting for him—a bowl of soft food that smelled like chicken and vegetables. His favorite.

He ate quickly while Benny got dressed. The boy looked nice too, Elmer thought. He had on a new polo shirt and his best jeans, and his wavy hair was just as shiny as Elmer's. Together, they made a great-looking team.

After the humans had their breakfast, the whole family set out for the gym. Only this time when they arrived, the parking lot, which usually had only a handful of cars, was packed. Signs out front announced CANINE TALENT SHOW! 10 A.M. ALL ARE WELCOME!

Inside, the gym was louder and more crowded than Elmer had ever seen it. Along the wall, where the staff usually kept stacks of spare equipment, were now rows of bleachers filled with people. And there were dogs of all different shapes and sizes walking around the main floor—golden retrievers, border collies, and whippets. There were even a few obstacles that Elmer had never seen. The jumps and ramps were higher, there were more poles to weave through, and two sets of seesaws.

"We have to go take our seats, sweetie," Marisol said, giving Benny a quick hug and Elmer a pat on his head. "Buena suerte."

"Yes, good luck out there, you two," added Reggie.

Elmer saw Benny craning his head in every

direction, he guessed searching for Kitts. He breathed a sigh of relief when he spotted her and Coda making their way toward them. Today, Coda had a handkerchief tied around her neck that matched Kitts's bright purple bandanna.

"Can you believe how crowded it is?" Kitts said. "There are even some kids from school in the stands." She nodded toward the third bleacher in, and Benny mouthed *Oh no*. Renee was there, waving and giving them a thumbs-up. Benny remembered she had been the only one to stand up for Elmer, so he guessed he didn't mind having her in the stands. But she'd brought A. J., Kyle, Martin, and Daisy.

Seeing the dread on his face, Kitts hurried to explain. "You aren't the only one who apologized to me in the past couple of days," she said. "Renee felt bad for ignoring me in the park too, and she called to say she was sorry. She remembered that we were both doing the talent show today, so she asked if she could come and bring her friends."

Benny groaned. "But what if we mess up and they make fun of us?"

"I don't think they will," Kitts said cheerily. "Not after they see what we've been up to!"

Elmer admired her positive outlook. Maybe she could help Benny to see things that way.

Benny shook his head. "I didn't know this many people would be here." He pulled at the neck of his shirt as if it would help him breathe better. Elmer heard a big *gulp* when Benny swallowed.

Soon a man in a dark suit took center stage

with a microphone. He announced that first the large dogs would go, followed by the medium dogs, and finally the small ones. But they would be picking the top three dogs overall based on how quickly they completed their tricks, how many mistakes they made, and how well they worked with their owners.

"Remember," he finished. "Everyone participating is already a winner!"

Benny and Kitts watched from the sidelines as a border collie named George tore through the course. He was fast, but he knocked over one of the poles during a jump and went through a tunnel in the wrong direction. Elmer felt comforted that the big dogs made mistakes too. But Benny seemed to get more and more nervous with each performance he watched.

After the last large dog completed his run, Benny announced that he needed some air.

Kitts and Coda followed him and Elmer outside.

"What's wrong?" Kitts asked.

Benny looked panicked. "I don't think I can do this!" he said. "You saw those dogs in there. They were all so good, and their owners really knew what they were doing. I feel sick." After a pause, he muttered, "I'm going to withdraw from the competition."

"What?" said Kitts, her mouth hanging open. "You can't do that!"

"But . . . but what if I forget which direction I'm supposed to run, or Elmer stops in the middle of the tunnel again? A. J. will never let me hear the end of it."

Kitts snorted. "Then laugh! Be part of the joke. This is supposed to be fun, remember? Everybody makes mistakes sometimes. It's not the end of the world. Besides," she continued, "you and Elmer have been working so hard. You just need to believe in yourself."

Elmer rubbed his head against Benny's leg and nibbled on his shoelace. It was Elmer's way of saying he believed in Benny too.

"You really think so?" he asked.

"I know so!" said Kitts.

Benny took a deep breath, and when he let it out, he seemed more relaxed. He even smiled. "Thanks, Kitts. You're the best."

"I know." She smiled and nodded back toward the gym. "Now, let's go give this crowd a show!"

Benny puffed up his chest and said, "Okay, I'm ready. How about you, Elmer?"

Elmer lifted his head and let out as forceful a bark as he could. *Ready!*

Benny shook Elmer's paw and said, "Then let's do this!"

Kitts and Coda were up first, and Benny cheered so loud, Elmer thought he'd lose his voice. Coda jumped through the tire swing better than any dog they'd seen that day. And Kitts called out all the commands perfectly. They completed the whole course in only twenty-five seconds. The crowd went wild, especially Kitts's parents. Benny even saw Renee standing up and cheering at the end of the bleachers.

Next up was the Pomeranian and then the

French bulldog. But finally, Elmer's turn had come. Benny walked him out to the starting position and waited for their cue. Then Benny shouted "Go!" and they were off!

Elmer galloped across the green felt, his long ears flying back behind him. He kept his eyes on Benny, who was jogging on his left, pointing the way. Soon he ran up the A-frame ramp where he had stopped to rest on the first day. But not now! He zoomed past the peak and padded quickly down the other slope without breaking his stride. And there was Benny, ready to guide him through the tube. It was so calm and blue inside that Elmer was tempted to stop and lay on his back, but he pictured Coda ahead of him and kept on running.

He cleared the low bar jump and the far

jump with ease. The crowd cheered each time he completed an obstacle, which only made him feel stronger and lighter. So when he came to the tire jump, he completely forgot to be afraid. "Now!" Benny cried, guiding him to the circle, and Elmer jumped, sailing through the air like a low-flying bird. The crowd went wild! They were so loud that he could hardly hear Benny instructing him to mount one end of the see-saw. But Elmer could tell what Benny wanted him to do just by the movement of his hands. He felt the board swing down as he crossed it, and then he saw the final challenge right ahead of him: the weaving poles.

"You can do it, boy," Benny shouted. "I believe in you!"

Elmer's heart soared as he dodged between

the poles, dipping in and out and in again. And then he crossed the finished line, and it was all over!

Right away, Benny swept Elmer into his arms and hugged his sleek body. "You did it, boy! Good job! I'm so proud of you. We might really have a shot to win this!"

Jeremy, Paige, and Persephone jogged over to congratulate him on a great run.

Soon, all the dogs who had performed in the talent show lined up next to their owners to await the results while the judges whispered quietly to one another. A couple of staff members wheeled out three platforms in different heights, the highest one in the center.

Then the announcer called for everyone's attention. It was time to reveal the winners!

"Good luck," Kitts whispered to Benny.

"Good luck to you," Benny whispered back.

"In third place," the announcer boomed, "George and his owner, Kaley Lynch!"

Kaley cried out in surprise and led her border collie out to the shortest podium. Paige handed Kaley a small trophy and put what looked like a bronze medal around George's neck. Everyone applauded.

"And in second place, we have Elmer, and his owner, Benicio Cruz!"

"Oh my goodness!" Kitts screamed. "You got second place! Congratulations!"

Benny looked around in disbelief for a moment. Then he put Elmer down and attached his leash. "Let's go take our bow, buddy!"

Elmer trotted alongside Benny and hopped

up onto the second-place platform. Jeremy walked over and handed Benny a beautiful silver-plated trophy with a figure of a leaping dog at the top. Then he bent down and placed a silver medal around Elmer's neck. "Who's a good boy?" Jeremy said, and gave Elmer a wink.

I am! Elmer thought happily.

Finally, the announcer lifted his microphone to say, "In first place . . . Coda and her owner, Kitts Galloway!"

Benny gasped. Then the crowd jumped to their feet and clapped and cheered. But no one clapped louder or longer than Benny. When Coda and Kitts took their place on the highest podium, Benny shouted, "Congratulations! You're the winner!"

"We both are!" Kitts answered, smiling from

ear to ear. Soon Kitts found herself cradling a huge three-tiered trophy, and Coda had a gold medal around her neck that matched her golden eyes. Elmer was happy for them, but he couldn't help feeling worried. He'd won second place, but would his family have been happier with him if he'd been first? He was so determined to be the best possible dog so that they'd be happy they'd adopted him, but he'd come up just a little bit short.

The minutes after that went by in a blur. Marisol and Reggie and Kitts's parents came over to take lots of pictures. Elmer got plenty of pets and cuddles from the trainers. Even Renee, A. J., Kyle, Martin, and Daisy came by to congratulate Benny and Kitts. Elmer watched closely as A. J. pulled Benny aside and said,

"Hey, I'm really sorry we made fun of your dog before. He's pretty cool."

"Thanks," said Benny, looking surprised. "I think so too."

"Maybe we can hang out sometime after school." He glanced pointedly at Kitts, Coda, and Elmer. "All of us."

Benny grinned warmly. "Sounds good," he said and gave A. J. a fist bump.

Elmer enjoyed more playtime with the other dogs. But soon he was all tuckered out. When Marisol found him lying on the green floor, struggling to stay awake, she smiled down at him and said, "You've had a big day. I think it's time to head home."

Elmer followed Benny and his parents to their car and watched as they placed the gleaming trophy and his silver medal into the trunk. As soon as he got settled into the back seat, he snuggled against Benny's legs and closed his eyes. For a little while, any worries he had about the talent show drifted away.

But when they reached the house and filed inside, Elmer couldn't help thinking about their second-place finish and wondering if Benny would be disappointed. He'd tried his hardest, but had it been enough to show Benny, Marisol, and Reggie that he was the very best dog for them? He didn't know.

Just in case, he tried to be extra neat when he ate his dinner that night, taking his time with the special food they served him so that none of it spilled on the floor. When Reggie mentioned that they'd be taking Elmer for a checkup at the veterinarian's office soon, Elmer didn't whimper at all. And when it came time to go to sleep, Elmer trotted right into his crate instead of asking for more last-minute treats.

But it wasn't until Marisol, Reggie, and Benny all gathered around his crate and sat on the floor that Elmer finally got the answer to the question he'd been asking himself all night.

"We have a little present for you," said Marisol, grinning at Elmer. She opened a small box and pulled out a shiny red collar with a heart-shaped silver tag at the end.

"It says, 'Elmer Cruz,'" Reggie explained.

"So you'll always know you're part of our family," finished Benny.

Elmer hesitated before he stepped forward. He sniffed at the box then, looked at Benny curiously.

Benny took the collar out of the box and fastened it around Elmer's neck. The silver tag shone like a star. "There," he said. "A perfect fit. Just like you're the perfect dog for us."

Just as he had done back at the dog rescue the day Marisol and Reggie came to take him home, Elmer completely forgot his manners and covered his new family in sideways kisses. He took turns jumping from Marisol's lap to Reggie's and then to Benny's, wiggling and wagging his tail, letting out excited yips, and pressing his wet nose against Benny's cheek. Benny laughed and said, "Okay, okay, we love you, too!"

Elmer had never been so happy in his whole life.

Danny & Ron's Rescue is a real place in South Carolina. Both professional horse trainers, Danny Robertshaw and Ron Danta have been rescuing dogs ever since 2005, when they started helping animals in Louisiana who had lost their homes because of Hurricane Katrina. But they didn't stop there. Soon they opened their hearts to dogs who had suffered in puppy mills and dog fights, who lived in shelters and junkyards, or who had been abandoned and were living on the streets. With assistance from veterinarians and groomers, the dogs in their care are spayed or neutered, vaccinated, dewormed, groomed, and microchipped. They are one of the only organizations that does not have an adoption fee but survives strictly on donations. But what makes Danny & Ron's Rescue truly unique is that the dogs live in their actual house and often sleep in their bed.

What was once a quiet home for two, including their horse stables, is now a safe haven for dogs who have been injured, abused, or neglected. There, not only do they receive organic food and a warm place to sleep, but they are loved and treated like part of the family until they are adopted by a family all their own. Since the founding of their rescue, Danny and Ron have aided more than thirteen thousand dogs. They now consider themselves guests in the dogs' house.

When Danny and Ron met Elmer Fudd in October 2017, he was living in a rural shelter in South Carolina and had severe medical challenges. His teeth had grown out of his mouth at a 90 degree angle, his jaw was broken, and he was missing the skin on the roof of his mouth,

making it impossible for him to chew or eat. As a result, he was extremely underweight. The infection in his eyes had become so serious, they thought he would be blind. He also had heartworm and a small bullet in his abdomen. Local veterinarians thought that the time and expense it would take to fix all Elmer's health problems made him a hopeless case.

Lucky for Elmer, that's when Danny and Ron came into his life. They raised the funds to get him the treatment he needed, which included seven surgeries. Even after many weeks of recovery, he still needed daily medications, eye drops, and special food. But Elmer not only survived, he thrived.

The whole staff at the dog rescue loved Elmer, but Valerie Moore, who brought Elmer

to Danny and Ron's attention in the first place;
took such a shine to the long-haired minia-
ture dachshund that she adopted him. Val's
husband, Bryan, is an active member of the
United States Air Force, and he describes
Elmer as the perfect military pet because he

"has the ability to show people that even with both physical and emotional scars we can never quit fighting. Even with a rough past, there is still a bright future, and every person and pet deserve that future!"

Finally in a safe, loving home, Elmer has proven himself to be a happy-go-lucky, funny, loyal dog who enjoys cuddling and meeting new people. But he still gets to spend time with his old friends at the dog rescue when Bryan is away on deployment. That has been helpful since Elmer continues to have daily medical needs and giving him his eye drops isn't always easy!

Valerie and Bryan also realized that Elmer had other talents aside from giving special sideways kisses. He loves to run, so they entered him in the Senior Division in the National Dachshund Races circuit. He competed in four states and finished third in the finals in Findlay, Ohio. Elmer was named the 2019 Military Pet of the Year & Mascot, a title he and his family used to raise awareness for animal rescue advocacy and military pet support services like Dogs on Deployment, a nonprofit organization that provides service members with the resources they need to be pet owners while serving in the military.

Last but not least, Elmer is a movie star! He appeared in the 2018 Netflix film *Life in the Doghouse*, a documentary about Danny, Ron, and the dog rescue they built together that saved Elmer's life. And what a life it has been! At twelve years old, Elmer is showing the world that senior dogs—even ones with tragic pasts like his—can go on to do incredible things and add joy and love to any home.

If you would like to find out more about Danny & Ron's Rescue and how you can help dogs like Elmer, visit their website at dannyronsrescue.org, or learn more about the documentary at lifeinthedoghousemovie.com.

Turn the page for a sneak peek of

Moose's Life in the Doghouse!

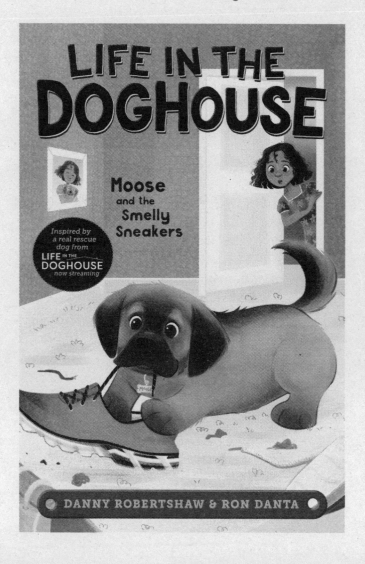

TODAY'S THE DAY!" Moose shouted as he tumbled through the house, announcing his good news to all the other dogs at Danny & Ron's Rescue. "I'm going home to a place called Rhode Island with my new family!"

"Congratulations, Moose," Cotton, a fluffy white poodle, called from behind a potted plant in the corner. Cotton was shy and often hid behind things. But she liked Moose enough to peek her head out.

"Gooood . . . fooor youuu . . . buddy," Buster the basset hound howled slowly in his deep voice. He lifted his droopy eyes and yawned. "That's . . . sooo . . . exciting."

"Would you keep it down? I'm trying to sleep," complained Amelia, lifting her head up from the cozy blanket tucked all around her. The small French bulldog spent most of her time curled up in a bed by the fireplace, and all the other dogs knew she liked her peace and quiet.

Moose skidded to a stop—which wasn't easy to do once he got going. With affection, people often said his short legs and wide body made him look like an adorable loaf of bread. But he moved pretty fast all the same. "Sorry, Amelia," he said.

She huffed and snuggled her snoot back under the warm wool blanket.

"Oh, don't pay her any mind. Amelia's always grumpy." Lucy, a bouncy border collie with a high-pitched bark and a spotted fur coat, approached Moose and lowered her nose to give his ear a quick lick. "We're all really happy for you. Even Amelia."

"Thank you, Lucy," Moose panted, wagging his stubby brown tail.

Moose was so busy talking to the other dogs and saying his goodbyes, he didn't even notice that Danny Robertshaw, one of the owners of the rescue, had come up behind him until he scooped Moose up into his arms.

"All right, little one. It's time to start your new life!" he said.

He settled Moose onto his shoulder and attached his leash as he carried Moose outside into the bright South Carolina sunshine.

In front of their redbrick home, Ron Danta, Danny's partner, was talking to the Delgado family. Moose had met them only a few days before, but Ron and Danny had known them for a long time through their participation in the horse shows. Anyone Danny and Ron had ever taught to ride a horse, or to lead a horse through a series of jumps, also knew that years ago, Danny and Ron had turned their home into a rescue for dogs, and sometimes cats. Since then, they'd taken in thousands of animals who needed their help, and now the house belonged more to the dogs than to them. Many of the dogs in their care ended up getting adopted by people in the horse show world. Lucky for Moose, he'd caught the eye of the Delgado family.

Lisette, a dark-haired woman with matching eyes and a heart-shaped face, stood next to two children flashing giant smiles. Rosa, about ten years old, barely reached her mother's waist—when she stood still, that is. Moose could tell she was excited by the way she kept jumping up and down on her open-toed sandals, her chin-length wavy hair bouncing right along with her. Her brother, Raymond, was taller and a little bit older, but he still had to squint as he gazed up at Ron, who towered over all of them.

"So what else could I do?" the woman said.

"Rosa's been begging for a puppy for years. When I spotted Moose, I decided it was finally time."

"Does it have to be a puppy, though? How about a snake?" asked the boy, holding his skinny arms far apart to show just how long he wanted the snake to be.

Lisette laughed. "Raymond, I don't think they have snakes here." She glanced at Ron and quirked one eyebrow up at him. "*Do* you?"

"Not that I know of," Ron answered with a chuckle.

About the Authors and Illustrator

DANNY ROBERTSHAW and **RON DANTA** are horse trainers and animal lovers who began helping dogs way before 2005. But when Hurricane Katrina hit, their rescue began in earnest as they saved over six hundred dogs from that national disaster. For their work during Katrina, they were 2008 ASPCA Honorees of the Year. Since then, Danny and Ron have used their personal home for Danny & Ron's Rescue, formed as a nonprofit 501(c)(3) that has saved over thirteen thousand dogs, all placed in loving homes. Danny, Ron, and their rescue were the subjects of the award-winning documentary *Life in the Doghouse*. They have also been featured on the *Today* show, *CBS Evening News*, the Hallmark Channel, *Pickler & Ben*, and several other TV shows. Their mission is a lifetime promise of love and care to every dog they take in. Visit them @DannyRonsRescue and at DannyRonsRescue.org, and learn more at LifeintheDoghouseMovie.com.

CRYSTAL VELASQUEZ is the author of several books for children, including the American Girl: Forever Friends series, the graphic novel *Just Princesses*, the Hunters of Chaos series, the Your

Life, but . . . series, and four books in the Maya & Miguel series. Her short story "Guillermina" is featured in Edgardo Miranda-Rodriguez's anthology *Ricanstruction: Reminiscing and Rebuilding Puerto Rico*. She holds a BA in creative writing from Penn State University and is a graduate of NYU's Summer Publishing Institute. Currently an editor at Working Partners Ltd., she lives in Flushing, Queens, in New York City and is the go-to dog sitter for all her friends. Visit her website at CrystalVelasquez.com, or follow her at Facebook.com/CrystalVelasquezAuthor or @CrystalVelasquezAuthor on Instagram.

LAURA CATRINELLA is an illustrator and character designer who loves to play with shapes and colors. She has fun creating a variety of different characters and people, all while being able to play around and tell a story with them. Usually, she can be found drawing at a park or coffee shop. Laura resides in British Columbia, Canada, and she spends most (all) of her time with her two mini dachshunds, Peanut and Timmy.

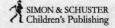

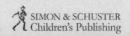